EARTHQUAKE

EARTHQUAKE

CHRISTOPHER LAMPTON

THE MILLBROOK PRESS
BROOKFIELD, CT
A DISASTER! BOOK

Cover photo courtesy of U.S. Geological Survey, Charles E. Meyer

Illustrations by Pat Scully

Photographs courtesy of National Geophysical Data Center, NOAA:
pp. 9, 43 (both); U.S. Geological Survey: pp. 14 (G.K. Gilbert), 26, 39
(R.E. Wallace), 46 (John K. Nakata); The Bettmann Archive: p. 15;
UPI/Bettmann Newsphotos: pp. 18, 20, 21, 24, 25; Paul Scott-Sygma:
p. 19; New York Public Library Picture Collection: p. 27; Historical
Pictures Service, Chicago: p. 32; NASA: p. 53; Superstock: p. 56.

Cataloging-in-Publication Data

Lampton, Christopher
Earthquake / by Christopher Lampton

p. cm.—(A Disaster! Book)
Bibliography p.   Includes index.
Summary: A graphic presentation of the causes and results of
earthquakes, including research methods scientists employ as
they investigate the origin, nature and control of this force.
ISBN 1-56294-031-7
1. Earthquakes. 2. Earth—Crust. 3. Plate tectonics.
4. Natural disasters. I. Title. II. Series.
551.22   1991

CONTENTS

EARTHQUAKE!

At first, it seems like a perfectly ordinary day. You get out of bed and step into the kitchen, where you eat a quick breakfast. Then you wash up and get ready for school. Finally, you walk to the front door and prepare to step outside.

And then it happens.

The floor beneath your feet begins to shake, ever so slightly.

You aren't even sure that something is wrong. Maybe a big bus is passing on the street outside. Or maybe somebody is stomping around on the floor upstairs.

The last thing that it could possibly be . . .

. . . is . . .

. . . an earthquake!

You push that thought out of your head and try to think about something else. Maybe the shaking will go away, you tell yourself, so that you won't have to think about it anymore.

But it doesn't go away, and after a few seconds you are pretty sure that it isn't being caused by a bus on the street outside. And you know that no one upstairs would be stomping around on the floor at this hour.

So you open the door and look outside, a little frightened. No sooner do you open the door than your dog comes tearing right past you, howling with terror! He bolts through the living room and disappears under the sofa, shivering with fear.

What could have frightened your dog that much? You look outside to see. The floor is still shaking, and when you step through your front door you discover that the ground outside is shaking, too. What's worse, the shaking is growing stronger. Now you're not sure if you can even keep standing. You grab the door but start to worry that your house might collapse.

Should you stay outside or run back inside? You're not sure, so you stay outside. You walk unsteadily along your front walkway. The ground seems to roll and lurch around you. You see other people making their way along the sidewalk, frightened expressions on their faces.

As you look down the street, you see an astonishing sight. A wave of concrete is rolling toward you, like the surf coming in off the sea. It's as though the solid ground has turned into an unsteady ocean, with a fierce storm churning up the waves!

Above it all, you hear a sound. It is a deep, hollow noise, like the howling of distant coyotes or wind whistling through a narrow canyon.

Then a crack opens up in the ground right in front of you! The very earth itself parts, like a giant door opening in the ground. The crack runs across your yard and into the middle of the street. A car coming down the street is unable to stop in time to avoid this sudden hole in the earth. The car plunges over the edge and falls into the crack, now several feet deep.

Streets can split open and close again,
trapping unwary motorists.

The driver of the car throws open the door and scrambles out. Just in time, too, because the crack closes itself as abruptly as it opened, crunching the car into scrap metal.

A house across the street suddenly collapses. The walls split apart and cave in like paper being crumpled in someone's hand. The house is now nothing more than a pile of rubble on the ground.

Finally, the trembling stops. The ground is no longer shaking. You look around at the pale, confused faces of the other people standing near you.

A sense of relief rushes over you. You have just been through an earthquake. The whole thing lasted only a little more than a minute.

And you survived it!

THE GROUND BENEATH OUR FEET

There are few things that seem more solid than the ground underneath our feet. We certainly don't expect the ground that we're walking on to start shaking or to open up beneath us. We build houses and offices and factories on it, fully expecting that they will stand for decades.

But the ground is less solid than it seems. Without warning, it can start to shake and tremble. Cracks can open in the earth, swallowing objects as large as automobiles. Houses can fall apart, tumbling to the ground in pieces. Bridges can collapse and trees can tip over.

When the ground shakes and shivers, we say that we are having an *earthquake.*

Earthquakes can happen anywhere, but they happen in some places more often than in others. In the United States, one of the places where earthquakes happen frequently is the city of San Francisco, California. Following are the stories of two great San Francisco earthquakes, both of which took place in the twentieth century.

11

THE SAN FRANCISCO EARTHQUAKE OF 1906

In 1906, San Francisco was still a frontier city. However, it was also the largest city in the American West, a great port sitting on the shores of the Pacific Ocean. It was populated by rowdy gamblers and refined millionaires alike. The houses of some of the wealthiest people in the nation looked down from hilltops onto saloons where cowboys still engaged in gunfights.

According to a report issued that year by the National Board of Fire Underwriters, San Francisco was also a firetrap. It was a "catastrophe waiting to happen." All that was needed was for something to start a fire under the city, and the whole place would burn to the ground.

On April 18, 1906, disaster struck.

A deep rumbling filled the air at 5:13 in the morning. The streets began to heave up and down. A policeman, on patrol in the hours before dawn, said that "the whole street was undulating [rising and falling]. It was as if the waves of the ocean were coming toward me, billowing as they came."

The earthquake lasted less than two minutes, but those minutes must have seemed like hours to the citizens of the town. Buildings began to fall. Cracks opened in the streets and sidewalks. Ships in the Pacific Ocean lurched violently up and down as giant waves suddenly came out of nowhere.

Most people were asleep when the earthquake started, but they were certainly awake by the time it ended. Thousands of San Franciscans poured out of their houses and into the streets. Hundreds, perhaps thousands, of others were trapped in the rubble. Many of the survivors worked long hours to rescue these unlucky ones, but not all could be saved.

The earthquake triggered fires all over the city, as lamps and stoves tumbled over and gas lines broke. The firetrap of a town began to burn, and it kept burning for three days. By the time the fire was over, more than 28,000 buildings had burned to the ground. Roughly 2,500 people died.

The world-famous opera singer Enrico Caruso was in San Francisco on the night of the earthquake. In the aftermath of the quake, he sang an aria (song) from the window of his hotel room to calm the members of the panicky crowd below—and probably to calm himself, too. Later, Caruso ran into the equally famous stage actor John Barrymore on his way to the harbor. Barrymore had been at a party when the earthquake struck. He was wearing black tie and tails. "Mr. Barrymore," Caruso told him, "you are the only man in the world who would dress for an earthquake!"

The best-selling author Jack London, who lived just outside of town on a farm, headed into the city immediately after the quake. He arrived in downtown San Francisco in time to witness the aftermath. Later, he wrote an article about it for a magazine. He de-

14

Above: The devastation from the great San Francisco earthquake of 1906 was nearly complete. Left: This picture of the effects from the earthquake shows how some of the houses have shifted out of position and are now leaning against neighboring structures.

■ 15

scribed the terrible devastation, but he was most impressed by the way the survivors had behaved. "Never in all San Francisco's history were her people so kind and courteous as on this night of terror," he wrote.

The devastation of the San Francisco earthquake of 1906 was indeed terrible. Yet the city began rebuilding almost immediately. Within only a few years, the city was not only as good as new, it was better. Most of the buildings that had burned down were replaced with new, stronger buildings by 1909. Within three years, the real estate value of the city was actually greater than it had been before the quake!

THE SAN FRANCISCO EARTHQUAKE OF 1989

At 5:04 P.M. on the afternoon of October 17, 1989, the third game of baseball's World Series was about to get under way in San Francisco's Candlestick Park. The two teams vying for the championship were the Oakland Athletics and the San Francisco Giants. Because both teams were based in the San Francisco area, some people were calling it the "Bay Bridge series." Fans would only have to drive across San Francisco Bay to see all of the games.

The two teams had just finished batting practice, and the stadium was already crowded with fans. Suddenly, the bleachers began to shake. A low rumbling sound echoed across the field. Blocks of concrete fell out of the stadium balconies, narrowly missing the people seated below. A television announcer barely had time to say the word "earthquake" before the World Series broadcast flickered off the air.

The earthquake lasted fifteen seconds. As the trembling died down, the World Series audience began to cheer. One held up a sign reading: THAT WAS NOTHING. WAIT TILL THE GIANTS BAT!

The scene at Candlestick Park, the home of the
Giants, after the 1989 earthquake forced Game 3
to end just as it was getting under way.

Nobody was hurt at Candlestick Park. Unfortunately, that wasn't true elsewhere in San Francisco. The worst disaster of the 1989 earthquake occurred in West Oakland, where the top half of a double-decker highway collapsed. The highway was crowded because it was the height of the rush hour. Dozens of cars were trapped in the rubble.

The worst disaster of San Francisco's 1989 earthquake occurred in West Oakland, with the collapse of the top half of a double-decker highway.

A fireman keeps watch in front of a destroyed
apartment building in the Marina District.
Right: A section of the Oakland Bay Bridge
collapses during the earthquake.

In the Marina District of San Francisco, buildings collapsed and fires broke out. In other parts of the city, building walls collapsed, in some cases falling on top of cars. More than 200,000 books fell off the shelves of a large downtown library, scattering over the floor.

Yet much of the city wasn't touched by the earthquake or was barely affected. The earthquake of 1989 wasn't nearly as bad as the earthquake of 1906. Experts estimate that the earlier quake had been 25 times more powerful.

Still, the results of the earthquake were costly and long lasting. Traffic in Oakland, for instance, was snarled by the loss of the double-decker highway for many months after the last echoes of the earthquake had died down.

EARTHQUAKES, EARTHQUAKES EVERYWHERE

San Francisco isn't the only city where earthquakes happen. They happen all over the world, and some of them have been a lot worse than the San Francisco quakes. Here are a few examples:

■ In 1988, a devastating earthquake struck Armenia in the Soviet Union, killing an estimated 25,000 people.

■ Mexico City was rocked by an earthquake in September 1985. More than 10,000 people died, and nearly 1,000 buildings were destroyed.

■ One of the most destructive earthquakes of modern times hit Tangshan, China, in 1976. More than 655,000 people were killed.

■ Chimbote, Peru, was the scene of an earthquake in May 1970. The quake triggered a landslide that buried an entire village. Nearly 70,000 people died.

■ The earthquake of 1923 is commemorated to this day by the citizens of Tokyo, Japan, in memory of the 143,000 lives lost to destructive ocean waves and fires.

■ 23

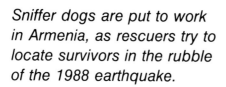

Sniffer dogs are put to work in Armenia, as rescuers try to locate survivors in the rubble of the 1988 earthquake.

The street shown here is Anchorage, Alaska's, main thoroughfare, right after the 1964 quake.

■ The 1920 earthquake in Kansu Province, China, covered such a wide area that ten cities were nearly destroyed and 200,000 people died.

■ An earthquake along the Sanriku coast of Japan in 1896 generated waves as tall as 115 feet. These waves killed 22,000 people.

■ The Charleston, South Carolina, quake of August 1886 was felt all over the eastern half of the United States. Eighty people were killed.

The earthquake in Charleston in 1886 is estimated to have caused $23 million in property damage.

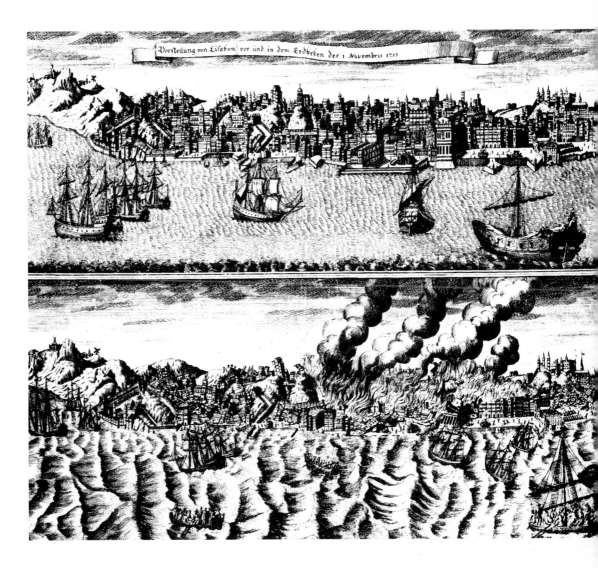

In 1755, Lisbon, Portugal, was struck by a massive quake, as this artist's engravings depict.

■ The 1872 earthquake in Owens Valley, California, may have been the most powerful in North America in recent centuries. Fortunately, the area was not heavily populated at the time, and few people were killed.

■ A violent earthquake in India in 1819 caused a large area of land to disappear permanently underwater. Another section of land, called the Allah Bund, was raised from beneath the water by the earthquake.

■ Over a two-month period in 1783, Calabria, Italy, was struck by six large earthquakes in a row. More than 180 towns and villages were affected, and almost 50,000 people died.

■ In 1737, an earthquake in Calcutta, India, killed an estimated 300,000 people.

■ An earthquake in 1692 caused the legendary pirate town of Port Royal, Jamaica, to sink into the ocean. As the years passed, people began to believe that the town had been a myth. Then, roughly two and a half centuries after it had sunk, underwater archaeologists uncovered it.

■ The earthquake that struck China's Shensi Province in 1556 may have been the worst natural disaster of all time. More than 830,000 people are estimated to have died.

There were many earthquakes before the sixteenth century, of course. But the records going back that far are poor, and it is difficult to be sure exactly what happened. We can be sure, however, that earthquakes have been around for almost as long as the planet earth has been orbiting the sun.

WHAT CAUSES EARTHQUAKES?

Why is it earthquakes happen? What makes the ground suddenly start to shake and rattle when it is usually so still?

Take a look at a map or a globe of the world, and you may find a clue. On a map, the continents and oceans of the world look steady and unmoving. But look carefully at the east coasts of North and South America and the west coasts of Europe and Africa. They look almost as though they would fit neatly together, like pieces of a jigsaw puzzle. The western bulge of Africa, for instance, would fit into the curve of Central America. Furthermore, the eastern bulge of South America would snuggle up nicely to the southwest coast of Africa.

Is it possible that these continents were once joined together? Could South America and Africa once have been a single continent? Did North America once fit into Europe? Did these continents, once a single landmass, break apart and drift away from one another? And could they still be moving?

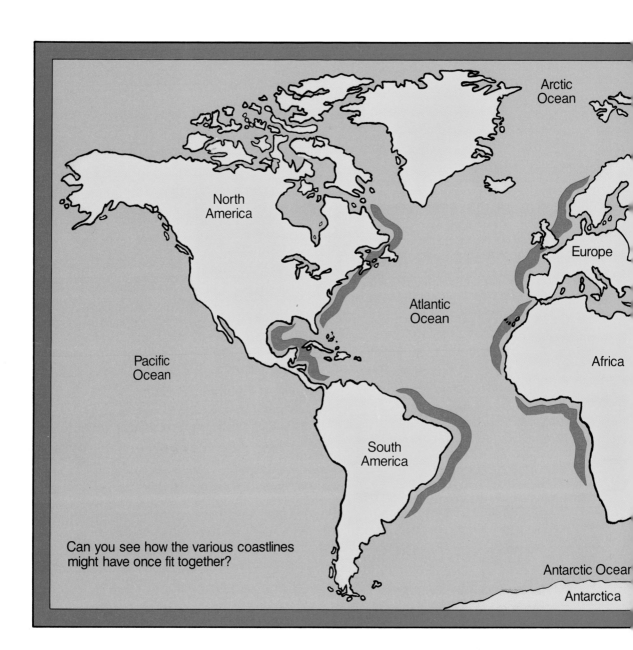

Can you see how the various coastlines
might have once fit together?

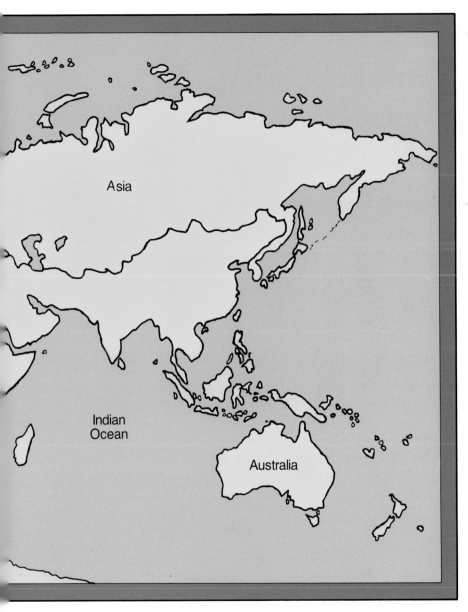

The Modern Continents

Asia

Indian
Ocean

Australia

The German geophysicist and meteorologist, Alfred Wegener (1880–1930), who first introduced the idea of continental drift.

This idea was first suggested centuries ago. But it wasn't until the early twentieth century that a German meteorologist (weather scientist) named Alfred Wegener popularized the idea of *continental drift.* Wegener gathered evidence showing that ancient fossils from South America bore a strong resemblance to ancient fossils in Africa. And he found geological features on these two continents—and in North America and Europe—that were so similar, it looked as though the continents had once been a single landmass.

Wegener suggested that all of the continents of the world were once part of a giant supercontinent that he called *Pangaea* (pan-GEE-uh). Millions of years ago, Wegener said, Pangaea must have broken apart, and the pieces drifted away to form the continents that we see today.

These ideas weren't immediately accepted by geologists, the scientists who study the landforms making up our planet. But in the late 1940s, geologists discovered evidence that the seafloor in the middle of the Atlantic Ocean is "spreading." Hot molten (melted) rock is rising up from inside the earth, forming new seafloor. This forces the continents of Europe and Africa to shift in one direction, while the continents of North America and South America are forced to move in the other direction. Wegener was right after all!

By the 1960s, the idea of continental drift was regarded as the most important new idea in geology. In fact, most of the other theories held by geologists had to be changed to fit into the theory of continental drift—or *plate tectonics,* as it soon came to be called. Tectonics is the science or art of constructing things out of smaller pieces. Plate tectonics is the way in which nature has created the surface of the earth from a number of smaller plates.

PLATE
TECTONICS

To see what continental drift has to do with earthquakes, let's look at the way in which the continents move about on the surface of the earth.

The planet earth is made up of several different layers, like an onion. The uppermost layer is called the *crust.* This is the layer on which we live, where we walk and drive cars and build buildings. There is even crust underneath the ocean.

The earth's crust is made up mostly of hard, rocky substances, though some of these substances have crumbled into dirt from years of exposure to wind and rain and the roots of plants. That crust is many miles thick (though the part under the ocean is thinner than the part on the land). Underneath the crust is a layer called the *mantle.* The mantle is about 1,800 miles thick. Below the mantle is the earth's *core,* which is made up of two layers called the *inner core* and *outer core.*

The inside of the earth is hot. The deeper you go, the hotter it gets. The mantle is so hot that it is made mostly of molten rock.

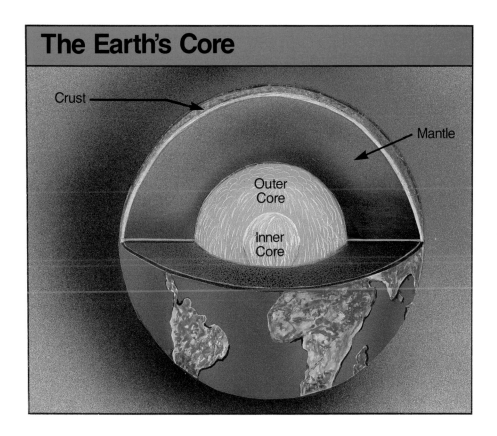

The Earth's Core

Crust

Mantle

Outer Core

Inner Core

The crust of the earth floats on this molten rock like boats float on water. The earth's crust is not all of one piece. In fact, it is broken up into fifteen pieces, called *plates.* Each of these plates can move independently of the others as it floats on the mantle.

Surprising things can happen where one plate meets another plate. Sometimes the first plate will ride over the top of the second plate, causing the second plate to sink down into the earth's mantle.

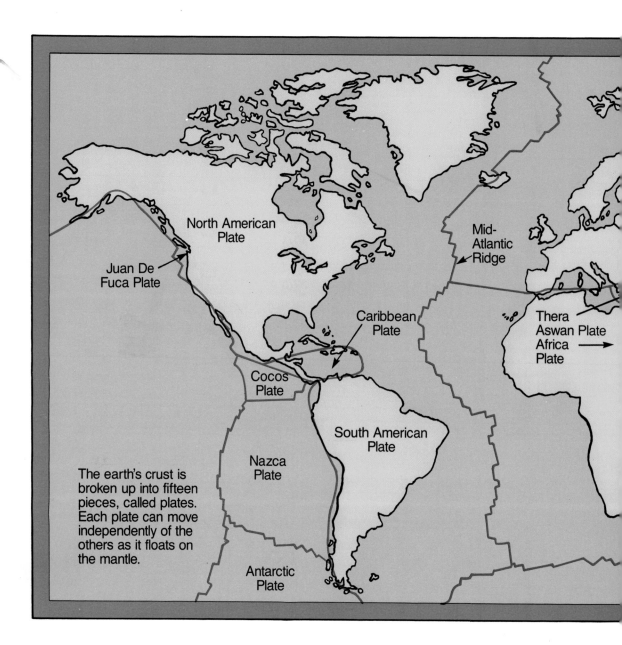

The earth's crust is broken up into fifteen pieces, called plates. Each plate can move independently of the others as it floats on the mantle.

North American Plate

Juan De Fuca Plate

Caribbean Plate

Cocos Plate

Nazca Plate

South American Plate

Antarctic Plate

Mid-Atlantic Ridge

Thera Aswan Plate Africa Plate

The Earth's Plates

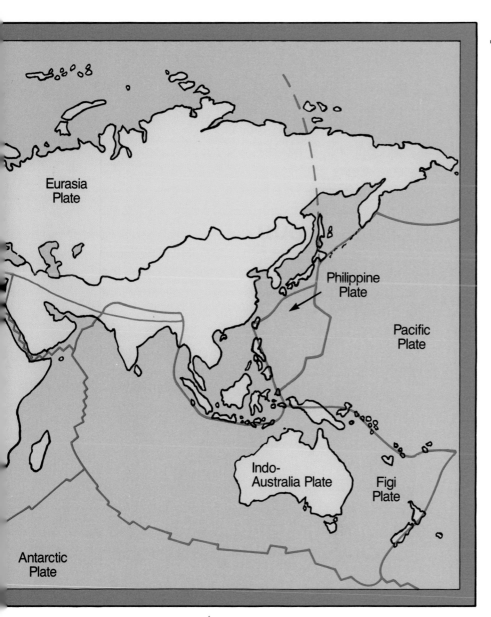

Eurasia Plate

Philippine Plate

Pacific Plate

Indo-Australia Plate

Figi Plate

Antarctic Plate

The place where this happens is called a *subduction zone.* In other places, two plates will crash together to form mountains. And in still other places, two plates will move along next to one another in a region called a *fault zone.* A typical fault zone contains a number of *faults,* unstable junctions or regions between the crustal materials in the two plates.

The North American continent is mostly on a single plate, called the North American plate. But a tiny portion of southern California and Mexico belongs to another plate, called the Pacific plate. These two plates come together in a long fault zone that includes the well-known San Andreas fault. The San Andreas fault runs through most of the state of California. The city of San Francisco lies almost directly on top of this fault. In some places you can actually see the San Andreas fault as a crack in the ground or a small valley or even as a lake (where a section of the fault zone has filled with water). In other places, it's invisible, buried beneath housing developments and shopping centers.

Like all of the plates that make up the earth's crust, these two plates are moving. But they are not moving in the same direction. The Pacific plate is moving northward up the North American plate. In fact, millions of years from now the city of Los Angeles (which is on the Pacific plate) will be next door to San Francisco (which is— just barely—on the North American plate).

When any two objects, such as these two crustal plates, rub up against one another, they create friction. This friction makes the plates stick together. However, the powerful forces inside the earth

An exposed section of the San Andreas fault.

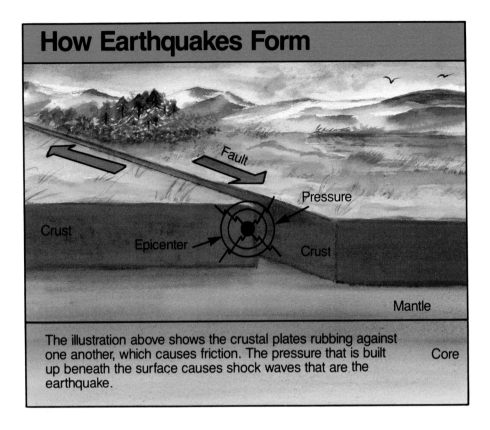

How Earthquakes Form

Fault

Pressure

Crust

Epicenter

Crust

Mantle

The illustration above shows the crustal plates rubbing against one another, which causes friction. The pressure that is built up beneath the surface causes shock waves that are the earthquake.

Core

that are causing the plates to move won't let them stick together for long. When enough pressure builds up inside the ground, the plates will move all at once, with a sudden jerking motion. Shock waves shoot out from the point at which the plates move. These shock waves are the earthquake. After a major earthquake, small movements in the rocks where the plates join together can cause additional tremors. These are known as *aftershocks*.

The reason that San Francisco has been the site of so many earthquakes is that it lies right on the San Andreas fault. However, there are many other areas along the San Andreas fault where earthquakes can occur as well. In addition, there are a number of smaller faults that surround the San Andreas fault, like branches on a tree. Each of these faults can also produce an earthquake. Quakes can also happen in the middle of a fault, but this kind of earthquake is much, much rarer.

There are other major faults around the world besides the San Andreas fault. On the opposite side of the Pacific plate, along the coast of Asia, earthquakes have been quite common. And some of these earthquakes have been far worse than the ones in California.

EARTHQUAKE DESTRUCTION

It's not hard to understand how earthquakes cause destruction. Many buildings aren't constructed to stand up to a violent shaking, and so they collapse almost immediately when the earth starts moving.

But earthquakes can cause destruction in other ways as well. One way is *liquefaction.* In many places, the ground isn't as solid as it looks. It may be made up of loosely packed gravel or sand. It may contain streams of underground running water. Ordinarily, this type of ground will support even a heavy building. But when an earthquake strikes, the sand particles collapse together and mix with the groundwater, turning into a liquid mass something like quicksand. Buildings can actually sink into the earth or founder like ships in a storm, rocking back and forth on the shifting sands.

Even more destructive than liquefaction is the legendary *tsunami.* (Sometimes the term "tidal wave" is incorrectly used to describe a tsunami.) These devastating ocean waves are created when the ocean bottom rises and falls from the shock of an earthquake.

This tsunami began in the Aleutian Islands and struck the beachfront in Hawaii. Waves in the area where it struck were over 20 feet high.

Liquefaction caused this house in Caracas to sink.

Tsunamis can rise to heights greater than a hundred feet. When they strike the shore, they carry an incredible amount of energy. They can destroy boats, smash dockside buildings, and flood the streets of a town in mere seconds. Some tsunamis consist of a half dozen or more waves in a row, each creating devastation when it reaches land.

On occasion, when the water from the tsunami has actually drained out the harbor, people have rushed to the shore to see this unusual spectacle. But then another wave rolls in and drowns the hapless sightseers!

DETECTING EARTHQUAKES

You might think it would be easy to detect an earthquake. Just wait until the ground starts shaking, and you've detected an earthquake. But some earthquakes are too small to be detected, and others occur in areas where few people live. And just because you can feel an earthquake doesn't mean you are standing right where the earthquake originated.

Scientists who study earthquakes are called *seismologists.* They like to know whenever an earthquake happens, so that they can study its effects and learn as much as they can about what causes earthquakes. To detect earthquakes, they use a *seismograph.*

A simple seismograph consists of a hanging weight, a moving strip of paper, and a pen attached to the weight. When the weight is steady, it will draw a straight line on the paper with the pen. But when the weight vibrates, it will draw a wavy line. Each line represents a single vibration. By attaching the weight to a rod going deep into the ground, seismologists can be sure that only earthquake vibrations will make it move. As a result of studying the vibrations of earthquakes, scientists have discovered that they come in three different kinds, *surface waves, P waves,* and *S waves.*

Surface waves are waves that move along the surface of the earth, just as water waves move along the surface of the water. P waves and S waves, on the other hand, move right through the earth itself. P waves (for "pressure waves") vibrate back and forth in the same direction in which the wave is traveling, like a wave running up and down in the type of toy called a slinky. S waves (for "shear waves") vibrate sideways (or perpendicular) to the direction in which the wave is traveling. You can imagine a P wave as squeezing and releasing the earth as it travels through it, while the S wave makes the earth wobble first to one side, then to the other.

Seismographs at the U.S. Geological Survey record earthquake waves whenever they happen within range of the instrument.

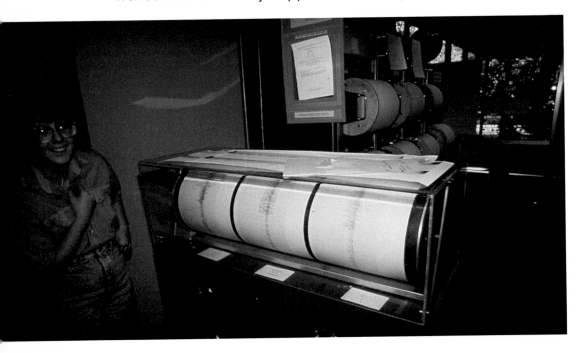

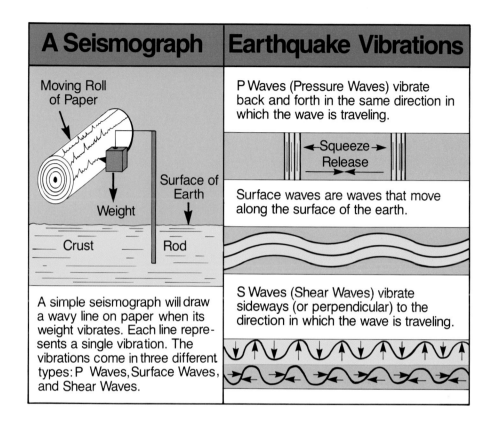

A Seismograph	Earthquake Vibrations

A Seismograph

Moving Roll of Paper

Weight

Surface of Earth

Crust   Rod

A simple seismograph will draw a wavy line on paper when its weight vibrates. Each line represents a single vibration. The vibrations come in three different types: P Waves, Surface Waves, and Shear Waves.

Earthquake Vibrations

P Waves (Pressure Waves) vibrate back and forth in the same direction in which the wave is traveling.

←Squeeze→
Release

Surface waves are waves that move along the surface of the earth.

S Waves (Shear Waves) vibrate sideways (or perpendicular) to the direction in which the wave is traveling.

P waves travel faster than the other kinds of waves. When an earthquake occurs, P waves are the first waves detected by distant seismographs; the S waves arrive later. The farther the seismograph is from the earthquake, the longer the time between the arrival of the P waves and the arrival of the S waves. In fact, this is how scientists tell how far away an earthquake is from a seismograph. They measure the time between the arrival of the P waves and the arrival of the S waves.

Although this tells seismologists how far away the earthquake is, it doesn't tell them in which direction the earthquake lies. To

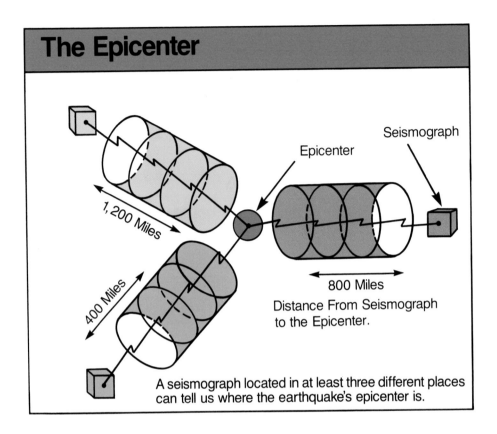

The Epicenter

1,200 Miles

Epicenter

Seismograph

400 Miles

800 Miles

Distance From Seismograph to the Epicenter.

A seismograph located in at least three different places can tell us where the earthquake's epicenter is.

pinpoint the earthquake exactly, they need seismographs in at least three different places. Once they know how far away the earthquake is from each of these places, they need only to look on the map to find a spot that is the right distance from all those places. Since there can be only one such spot, this must be where the earthquake originated.

The point from which an earthquake originates is known as its *epicenter.* This is not necessarily the place where the most destruction takes place, however. The effects of an earthquake can travel for many hundreds of miles.

MEASURING EARTHQUAKES

There are two systems that we use to measure earthquakes. They are the *Mercalli scale* and the *Richter scale.* These aren't actual physical scales, like the ones you use to measure your weight. Rather, they are both ways of using numbers to describe the strength of earthquakes.

The Mercalli scale was developed in 1902 by the Italian geologist Giuseppi Mercalli. It is based on the observed physical effects of the earthquake and is measured in Roman numerals. An earthquake that is so gentle that no one even feels it, for instance, gets a I on the Mercalli scale. An earthquake that can be felt only by people sitting on the upper floors of a tall building gets a II. At the other end of the scale, an earthquake that causes general panic and heavy destruction gets a IX, and earthquakes that create nearly total destruction rate an XI or a XII. (These are the highest rankings on the Mercalli scale.)

The Richter scale, proposed in 1935 by the American physicist Charles Richter, is more precise than the Mercalli scale. It is based on seismograph readings. The Richter scale starts at zero (no earthquake at all) and goes as high as is necessary to describe an

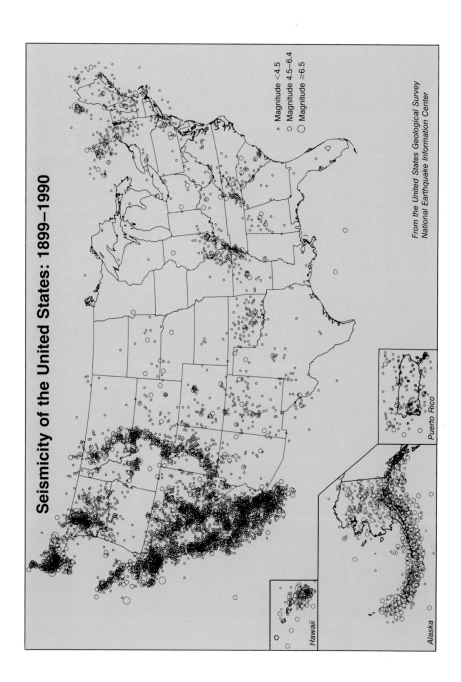

Seismicity of the United States: 1899–1990

Magnitude <4.5
Magnitude 4.5–6.4
Magnitude ≥6.5

From the United States Geological Survey
National Earthquake Information Center

Puerto Rico

Hawaii

Alaska

earthquake. (In practice, no earthquakes higher than 9.0 have ever been detected.)

Each number on the Richter scale represents an earthquake ten times as powerful as the number below it. Therefore, an earthquake that receives a 2 on the Richter scale would be ten times more powerful than an earthquake that receives a 1.

The San Francisco earthquake of 1989 (now known as the Loma Prieta quake, after the town where its epicenter was located) registered 6.9 on the Richter scale. The earlier San Francisco quake of 1906, however, was an 8.3 quake. This is 1.4 higher on the scale than the 1989 quake, which means that it was between 10 and 100 times more powerful. (As a rough estimate, we can say that the 1906 quake was about 25 times more powerful than the 1989 quake.)

PREDICTING EARTHQUAKES

If we could predict earthquakes in advance the way that we predict, say, hurricanes in advance, we could save many lives. People in the area where the earthquake was expected could be evacuated. Then only buildings would be destroyed.

Alas, there is no foolproof way yet to predict earthquakes. Scientists frequently know *where* earthquakes are going to happen, but they usually don't know *when*—at least not accurately enough to allow the area to be evacuated.

The most common method of predicting earthquakes today is the *seismic gap method.* The idea behind this method is simple. Pressure builds up along a fault over time. An area along a fault that hasn't had an earthquake in a while is more likely to have one than an area that has had a recent earthquake, because more pressure will have built up.

Most seismologists believe that the next big earthquake in the United States will be somewhere in southern California. Why? Because there haven't been any big earthquakes there recently. A lot

Satellites can now measure tiny shifts in the earth's plates, allowing for more opportunity to predict earthquakes.

of pressure has built up along that part of the San Andreas fault. The most likely way that this pressure will be released is in a large earthquake or even a series of large earthquakes. Unfortunately, there's no way to know when this will happen. It may be tomorrow—or any time in the next fifty years. More than fifty years is unlikely, however, because the pressures building up inside that part of the fault will become too great.

Scientists have had occasional good luck in predicting earthquakes. In 1975, scientists in China predicted an earthquake in the town of Haicheng only five hours before it happened. But it allowed time for millions of people to be evacuated. Doubtlessly, this prediction saved many lives. This is the only earthquake that Chinese seismologists have predicted with such accuracy, however.

In the late 1980s, American geologists began burying special measuring devices in the ground along the San Andreas fault in central California. These devices are intended to measure movements along the fault. Using these measurements, scientists may be able to gauge the amount of stress building up before it causes an earthquake. Perhaps someday such devices will give us accurate warnings of upcoming earthquakes.

What should you do if you find yourself caught in an earthquake? First of all, don't panic. Most earthquakes are fairly mild and don't cause much damage.

The worst danger in an earthquake is falling debris. If you are inside a building, go someplace where you'll be safe from anything that might fall. Sit under a table, for instance, or stand in the frame of a doorway. If you're outside, don't go near any buildings. If you're in a car, have the driver pull over to the side of the road until the earthquake passes.

PREVENTING EARTHQUAKES

If we could predict earthquakes, we could evacuate the areas where they were going to happen and save lives. If we could actually *prevent* the earthquakes, we could not only save lives but also prevent millions of dollars worth of damage to property. But is there any way to stop an earthquake?

No one knows for sure, but it may be possible. One method may be to "grease" the faults where the earthquakes occur. This would allow the plates to move smoothly against one another without building up the pressure that causes earthquakes.

Seismologists have already experimented with earthquake-control wells. These are pits dug in the earth along a fault that can be filled with water to make the fault more "slippery." Some scientists have suggested that one day such wells may be dug all along the San Andreas fault. Every time water (or some other fluid) is injected into such a well, it would create a mini-earthquake, too small to cause damage but large enough to let off some of the pressure from the fault.

Perhaps the best method of preventing earthquake disasters is to not build cities near faults in the earth in the first place. Unfortunately, many of the world's largest cities have already been built either near faults or directly on top of them, and the people who live in those cities are understandably reluctant to move out. The second best method of preventing disaster, then, may be to make sure that the buildings in these cities are constructed in such a way that they can withstand the shock of a powerful quake. In fact, many of the buildings in San Francisco have already been built this way, but not all of them. And until earthquake-prone cities have been made completely earthquake-proof, the death of innocent citizens and the destruction of expensive property will just keep on happening.

This spectacular aerial view of San Francisco shows a city more prepared to withstand earthquake shocks than ever before. But no one knows if it will be enough.

GLOSSARY

aftershocks—the tremors that follow a major earthquake.

continental drift—the movement of the continents in the Eastern Hemisphere and the continents in the Western Hemisphere away from each other. This movement is caused by the motion of the plates that make up the earth's crust.

core—the innermost portion of the planet earth.

crust—the outermost layer of the planet earth; a rocky layer floating on top of the semi-liquid mantle below.

epicenter—the point from which an earthquake originates.

fault—an unstable section of earth where parts of two different plates meet.

fault zone—an area where two plates meet one another on the earth's surface.

inner core—the innermost portion of the earth's core.

liquefaction—the manner in which loose-packed ground and groundwater can combine during an earthquake. Together they can form a quicksandlike semi-liquid that can swallow houses and other objects.

mantle—the semi-liquid layer directly below the earth's outer crust.

outer core—the outermost portion of the earth's core.

Pangaea—pronounced "pan-GEE-uh," the supercontinent that existed on earth millions of years ago when all of the major landmasses of the earth's crust had come together to form a single landmass.

plate tectonics—the way in which the plates that make up the earth's crust gradually rearrange themselves over long periods of time. The word *tectonics* refers to the art or science of constructing things out of smaller pieces.

plates—the independently moving pieces of the earth's crust.

P waves—short for "pressure waves"; earthquake waves that travel through the center of the earth, vibrating back and forth in the same direction in which the wave is traveling. In effect, a P wave squeezes and releases the earth it has traveled through.

seismic gap method—a method of predicting upcoming earthquakes by noting which fault zones have gone the longest without producing an earthquake.

seismograph—a device for detecting earthquake vibrations.

seismologist—a scientist who studies earthquakes.

subduction zone—a place where one plate of the earth's crust descends beneath another and is swallowed up by the hot mantle.

surface waves—earthquake waves that move along the surface of the earth, much as water waves move along the surface of water.

S waves—short for "shear waves"; earthquake waves that travel through the center of the earth, vibrating sideways, or perpendicular, to the direction in which the wave is traveling. In effect, an S wave causes the surrounding earth to wobble from one side to the other as it passes through.

tsunami—a large water wave caused by earthquake vibrations on the ocean floor; also informally called a "tidal wave."

RECOMMENDED READING

Asimov, Isaac. *How Did We Find Out About Earthquakes?* New York: Walker, 1978.

Kiefer, Irene. *Global Jigsaw Puzzle: The Story of Continental Drift.* New York: Atheneum, 1980.

Lambert, David. *Earthquakes.* New York: Franklin Watts, 1982.

Radlauer, Ed and Ruth. *Earthquakes.* Chicago: Children's Press, 1987.

Rutland, Jonathan. *The Violent Earth.* New York: Warwick Press, 1980.

Vogt, Gregory. *Predicting Earthquakes.* New York: Franklin Watts, 1980.

INDEX